For Chris, Clio, and Isla—who make everything fun.
—D.P.

For Eli, because you're you.
—M.B.

 Published in the United States by Doubleday, an imprint of Random House Children's Books, a division of Random House LLC, a Penguin Random House Company, New York.

Doubleday and the colophon are registered trademarks of Random House LLC.

Visit us on the Web! randomhousekids.com

Educators and librarians, for a variety of teaching tools, visit us at RHTeachersLibrarians.com

Library of Congress Cataloging-in-Publication Data
Petty, Dev.
I don't want to be a frog / by Dev Petty ; illustrated by Mike Boldt. — First edition.
pages cm.
Summary: A frog who yearns to be any animal that is cute and warm discovers that being wet, slimy, and full of bugs has its advantages.
ISBN 978-0-385-37866-6 (trade) — ISBN 978-0-375-97334-5 (lib. bdg.) —
ISBN 978-0-375-98234-7 (ebook)
[1. Self-acceptance—Fiction. 2. Frogs—Fiction. 3. Animals—Fiction.] I. Boldt, Mike, illustrator.
II. Title. III. Title: I do not want to be a frog.
PZ7.P448138Iaaf 2015 [E]—dc23 2014012949

MANUFACTURED IN CHINA
10 9 8 7 6 5 4 3 2 1
First Edition

Random House Children's Books supports the First Amendment and celebrates the right to read.

I DON'T WANT TO BE A FROG

written by Dev Petty
illustrated by Mike Boldt

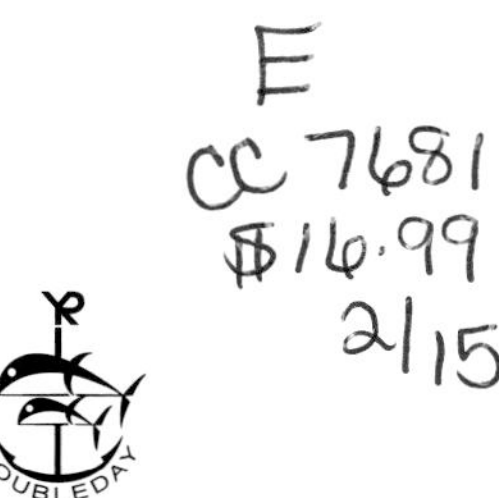

DOUBLEDAY BOOKS FOR YOUNG READERS

I want to be a

CAT.

You can't be a CAT.

Why not?

Because you're a FROG.

I don't like being a Frog.

It's too

Wet.

Well, you can't be a Cat.

I want to be a
Rabbit.
You can't
be a Rabbit.

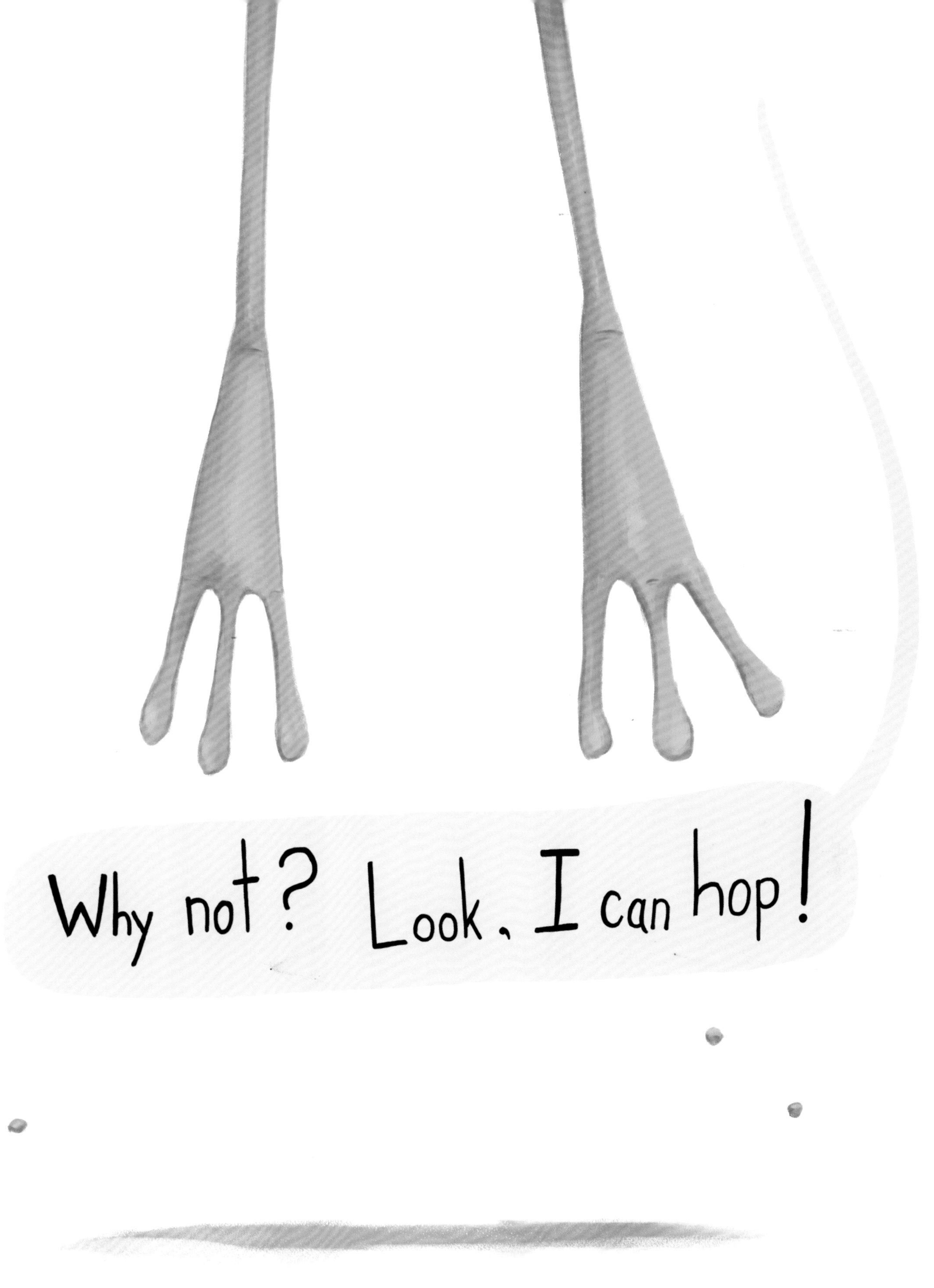

Why not? Look. I can hop!

Besides, what's wrong with being a Frog?

I don't like being a Frog. It's too **Slimy**.

That may be. But you can't be a Rabbit.

I want to be a Pig.

You can't be a Pig.

Why not?

Most of all because you're a Frog. But also because you don't have a curly tail or eat garbage.

I can eat garbage.

Everyone says that until they eat garbage. Sorry, you can't be a Pig.

I want to be an
Owl.

Of course you want to be an Owl!

Being an Owl is the greatest thing ever.

Boy, would you love being an Owl.

So can I be an Owl, then?

No, of course not!

Why not?

1. You don't have wings.

2. You don't look wise.

3. You can't turn your head all the way around.

4. YOU ARE A FROG.

What's wrong with being a Frog anyway?
Too much Bug Eating.
I see.
But still, NO being an Owl for you.

Why so glum?
I don't want to be a Frog.
What do you want to be, then?

Not a Frog. I want to be a

Cat or a **Rabbit** or a **Pig**

or an **Owl**.

Something cute and warm.

I'm going to let you in on a little secret....

I LOVE eating Cats.
I love eating Rabbits
and Pigs and Owls too.
And I am pretty hungry.
I might just go gobble
some up right now.
That's terrible!
It's who I am.
But guess the one
thing I never eat.

Badgers?
2 dozen
PREMIUM QUALITY
ORGANIC BADGERS
Nooo, I eat Badgers. Lots of Badgers.

Frogs?
BINGO.
Why don't you eat Frogs?
Because they are too wet and slimy and full of Bugs.
Oh. So it's good to be a Frog?

Yup.
I guess you can't fight nature. We are what we are.
You are a fierce hunter.

And you are a

Wet, Slimy, Bug-Eating,

very lucky Frog.

You should just be happy you're not a **Fly**.

What's wrong with being a FLY?